SHARE A STORY

THE OTHER DAY I MET A BEAR

Introduction

One of the best ways you can help
your children learn and learn to read
is to share books with them. Here's why:

• They get to know the **sounds**, **rhythms** and **words**
used in the way we write. This is different from how we
talk, so hearing stories helps children learn how to read.

• They think about the **feelings** of the characters
in the book. This helps them as they go about
their own lives with other people.

• They think about the **ideas** in the book. This helps
them to understand the world.

• Sharing books and listening to what your children
say about them shows your children that you care
about them, you care about what they think
and who they are.

Michael Rosen

Michael Rosen
Writer and Poet
Children's Laureate (2007-9)

For my father

First published 2001 by Walker Books Ltd
87 Vauxhall Walk, London SE11 5HJ

This edition published 2011

10 9 8 7 6 5 4 3 2 1

Illustrations © 2001 Russell Ayto
Concluding notes © CLPE 2011

The right of Russell Ayto to be identified as illustrator of this work
has been asserted by him in accordance with the Copyright,
Designs and Patents Act 1988

This book has been typeset in Beniolo

Printed in China

British Library Cataloguing in Publication Data:
a catalogue record for this book is available from the British Library

ISBN 978-1-4063-3504-0

www.walker.co.uk

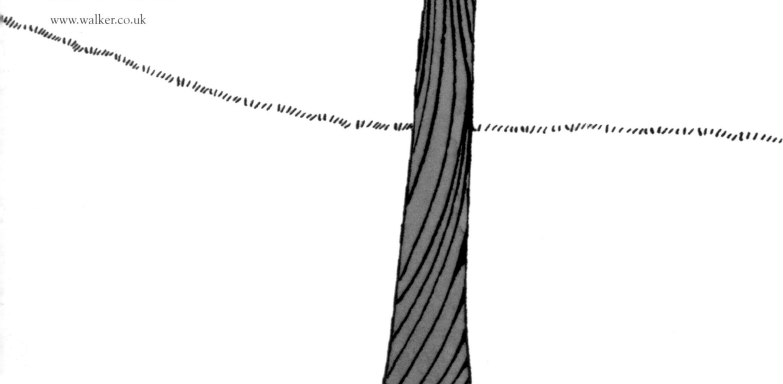

THE OTHER DAY I MET A BEAR

A TRADITIONAL TALE

ILLUSTRATED BY RUSSELL AYTO

WALKER BOOKS
AND SUBSIDIARIES
LONDON • BOSTON • SYDNEY • AUCKLAND

The other day I met a bear

out in the woods, away out there.

He looked at me. I looked at him.

He sized up me.   I sized up him.

He said to me, "Why don't you run?
I see you don't have any gun."

I said to him, "That's a good idea.

Come on now, feet, get out of here!"

And so **I** ran away from there,

but right behind me ...

And then **I** saw ahead of me

a great big tree. Oh, glory be!

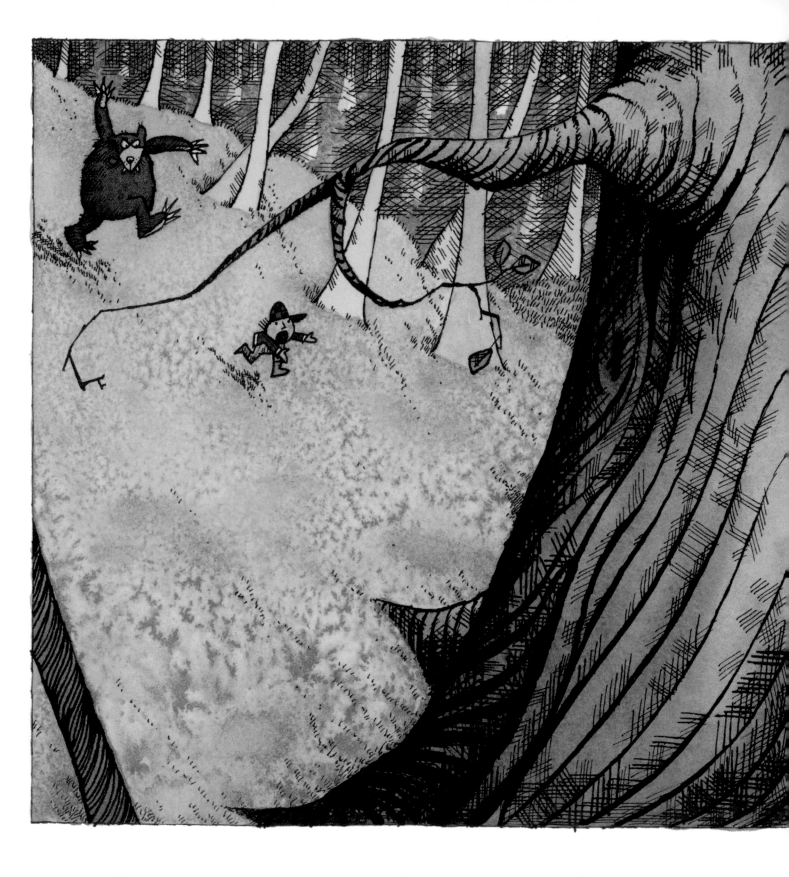

The lowest branch was ten feet up.

I'd have to jump and trust my luck!

And so I jumped

into the air ...

but missed the branch

away up there.

But don't you fret and don't you frown –

I caught that branch on the way down!

That's all there is. There ain't no more.

Unless ...

Sharing Stories

Sharing stories together is a pleasurable way
to help children learn to read and enjoy books.
Reading stories aloud and encouraging
children to talk about the pictures and join in
with parts of the story they know well are
good ways to build their interest in books.
They will want to share their favourite books
again and again. This is an important part
of becoming a successful reader.

The Other Day I Met a Bear is a humorous traditional song. It is told with comic strip style illustrations that bring out the drama and excitement of a chase and lucky escape – until next time. Here are some ways you can share this book:

• Talking together about the book – the words and the pictures – is an important way for children to tell you what they understand about the story and to ask questions. It helps to make it more meaningful and enjoyable.

• After reading the book aloud several times, you can encourage children to join in by leaving spaces for them to finish the rhyme. It's good fun and helps them to listen to the sounds and rhythms of rhymes and songs.

• Rhymes are a powerful way for children to understand the match between the words they say and the letters they see on the page. They help children to notice that some words sound and look alike.

• Talking about the book gives children the chance to say what they like about it and tell you about other stories or experiences it reminds them of.

• Encourage children to tell the story about meeting the bear in their own words. They can use the pictures to help them.

SHARE A STORY
A First Reading Programme
From Pre-school to School

Sharing the best books makes the best readers

WALKER BOOKS

www.walker.co.uk